Angelika Glitz · Annette Swoboda

Millie's Secret

CAT'S Whiskers

Millie was grinning from ear to ear.

"I've got a secret," she told Rudi.

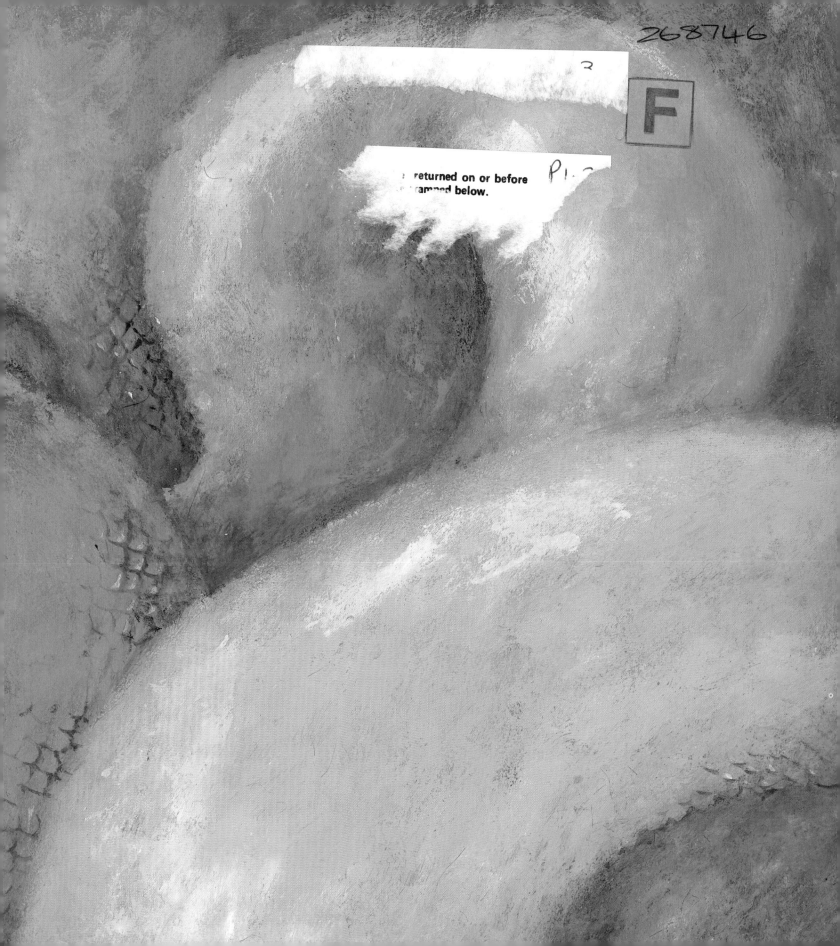

268746

F

returned on or before
...amped below.

For Marie,

and for Ralph

and for all the secrets of the world

This edition first published in 2000 by
Cat's Whiskers
96 Leonard Street
London EC2A 4XD

Cat's Whiskers Australia
14 Mars Road
Lane Cove
NSW 2066

ISBN 1 90301 208 2 (hbk)
ISBN 1 90301 209 0 (pbk)

Originally published by K. Thienemanns Verlag, Stuttgart, Vienna, Berne
Copyright © K. Thienemanns Verlag 1998
English text copyright © Cat's Whiskers 2000

A CIP catalogue record for this book is available from the British Library

Printed in Belgium

"What is it?" asked Rudi.
"I'm not telling," said Millie.
"Secrets aren't for telling!"

It's just as well I'm champion at
finding them out, Rudi thought.
He was so excited at the idea of a
secret that his feet got all tangled
up in the skipping rope.

...or a slimy toad?

Rudi suggested all sorts of wonderful secrets, but Millie just laughed.

"No, no, no," she said. "You'll have to keep on guessing!"
And off she ran.

Rudi tried to follow her, but he was all tied up in rope.

"Millie's got a secret," he told
his Mum when he got home.
But his Mum was on the 'phone;
she couldn't help.

Rudi would just have to
find out by himself.

That afternoon, Rudi met Millie
by the boating pond.

"I bet it's a Viking helmet," he said.
Millie laughed. "Don't be silly!
It's a thousand times bigger,
a thousand times heavier
than that!"

A thousand times
bigger than a Viking helmet...

a thousand times
heavier than a Viking helmet...

What on earth could it be?

Was it a huge snake?

...or pirate treasure?

...or an octopus
with eight arms?

...or an alien from outer space?

In the morning Rudi still had no idea
what the secret was. So he put on his
vampire suit and flew to the sandpit.

"Woo-oo-ooh!" he wailed in a scary
vampire voice. "Tell me your secret,
or I'll bite you!"

But Rudi had forgotten to put in his vampire teeth, silly thing! Millie recognised him straightaway.

"All right, then," said Rudi.
"If you tell me, I'll give you
my two biggest marbles."
But Millie didn't
want the marbles.
Instead, she gave
Rudi a clue.

"It's an animal,"
she whispered as she
jumped down from the swing.

So it's a big, heavy animal, is it? thought Rudi. I wonder if it's got two large ears...

...and perhaps a very long nose?

"Millie's most probably got an elephant,"
he told everyone at tea-time. "And all I've got is a guinea-pig."

Then Millie appeared.
"Come on," she said,
"come and see my secret.
Secrets are more fun
if you share them
with a friend."

So Millie and Rudi went along the road...

...through the village...
...across the field...

...up and down the seven hills...

...and into the wood.

Finally, Millie stopped.

"Shhh... There it is!"

"But that's not an elephant, that's
just a rock! A boring old grey
rock!" said Rudi in disgust.
And he stomped off in a huff.
"Wait," cried Millie,
"wait till I show you..."

But it was too late.
Rudi had disappeared
back into the wood.

So Millie climbed onto
the rock by herself...

...the only rock in the whole world
with such a very special...

secret!

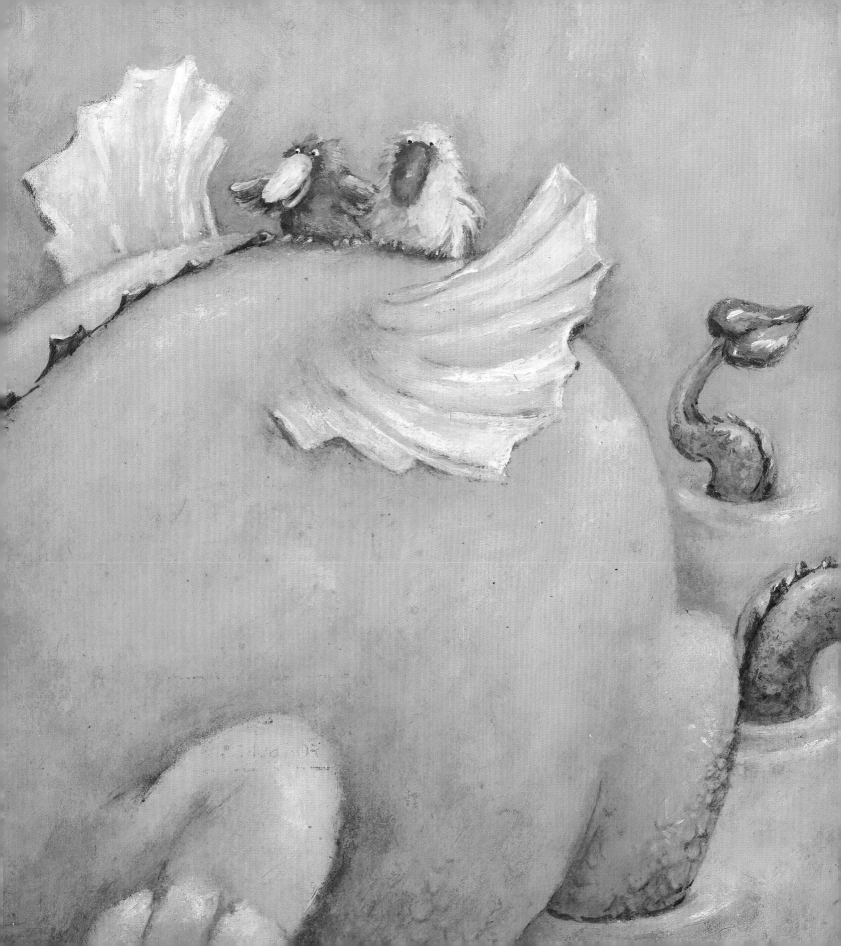